Out of nowhere
a great white stallion appeared.
He pranced and whinnied.
He swished his long white tail.
He stood on his hind legs,
his white mane flying. . . .

THE WHITE STALLION

The White Stallion

by ELIZABETH SHUB
pictures by RACHEL ISADORA

A Bantam Skylark Book®
Toronto / New York / London / Sydney / Auckland

*This edition contains the complete text
of the original hardcover edition.*
NOT ONE WORD HAS BEEN OMITTED.

RL 2, 007–009

THE WHITE STALLION
*A Bantam Book / published by arrangement with
Greenwillow Books*

PRINTING HISTORY
Greenwillow edition published September 1982
*The story of the white stallion is retold from James Frank
Dobie's Tales of the Mustang.*
*Bantam Skylark edition / September 1984
11 printings through February 1988*

*Bantam Books are published by Bantam Books, a division of Bantam
Doubleday Dell Publishing Group, Inc. Its trademark, consisting of the
words "Bantam Books" and the portrayal of a rooster, is Registered in
U.S. Patent and Trademark Office and in other countries. Marca
Registrada. Bantam Books, 666 Fifth Avenue, New York, New York 10103.*

PRINTED IN THE UNITED STATES OF AMERICA

CW   20 19 18 17 16 15 14 13 12

For J.B.

—E. S.

For Maureen and Jim

—R. I.

The
White Stallion

This is a true story, Gretchen.
My grandmother Gretchen,
your great-great-grandmother,
told it to me.
She was as young as you are
when it happened.
She was as old as I am
when I heard it from her.

3

It was 1845. Three families
were on their way West.
They planned to settle there.
They traveled in covered wagons.
Each wagon was drawn
by four horses.
Conestoga wagons they were called.

Gretchen and her family
were in the last wagon.
Mother and Father sat
on the driver's seat.
The children were inside
with the household goods.

Bedding, blankets, pots and pans,
a table, chairs, a dresser
took up most of the space.
There was not much room left
for Trudy, John, Billy, and Gretchen.
Gretchen was the youngest.

Behind the wagon
walked Anna, their old mare.
She was not tied to the wagon
but followed faithfully.
She carried two sacks
of corn meal on her back.

It was hot in the noonday sun.
The children were cranky and bored.
The wagon cover shaded them,
but little air came in
through the openings
at front and back.

John kicked Billy.
Billy pushed him,
and he bumped Gretchen.
Trudy, the oldest,
who was trying to read,
scolded them.

Their quarrel was interrupted
by Father's voice.
"Quick, everybody, look out!
There's a herd of mustangs."
The children clambered
to the back of the wagon.

In the distance
they could see the wild horses.
The horses galloped swiftly
and, in minutes, were out of sight.

"Look at Anna," John said.
The old mare stood rigid.
She had turned her head
toward the mustangs.
Her usually floppy ears
were lifted high.
The wagon
had moved some distance
before Anna trotted after it.

13

It was hotter than ever inside.
"Father," Gretchen called,
"may I ride on Anna for a while?"
Father stopped the wagon
and came to the back.

He lifted Gretchen onto the mare.
The meal sacks
made a comfortable seat.
He tied her securely
so that she would not fall off.

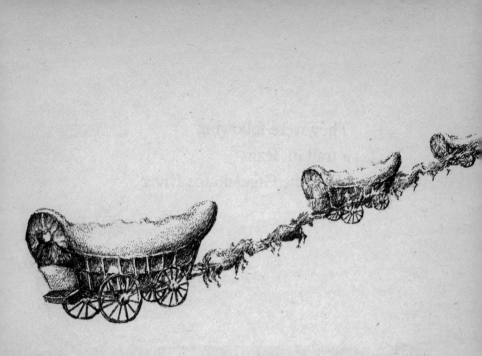

As they moved on,
Gretchen fell asleep,
lulled by the warmth
of the sun.

They were following
a trail in Texas
along the Guadeloupe River.

The rear wheel
of the first wagon
hit a boulder,
and the axle broke.
The whole train stopped.

Anna strayed away,
with Gretchen sleeping
on her back.
No one noticed.
The travelers made camp.
Children were sent for firewood
and for water from the river.
The women prepared food.

It was not until the axle
had been fixed
and they were ready to eat
that Gretchen and Anna
were missed.

The men tried to follow
the mare's tracks
but soon lost them.
It was getting dark.
There was nothing to do
but remain where they were.
They would search again
at the first sign of light.

Faithful Anna, they thought,
would return.
She probably had discovered
a rich patch of mesquite grass.
She would come back
when she had eaten
all she wanted.

Gretchen awoke to the sound
of lapping.
Anna was drinking noisily
from a stream.
A short distance away
stood a herd
of ten or twelve wild horses.
They were brownish in color.
Some had darker brown stripes
down their backs.
Others had dark markings
on their legs.
They were mares.

After Anna had finished drinking,
she moved toward them.
And they walked forward
as if to greet her.
When they came close,
they neighed and nickered.

They crossed necks with Anna,
nuzzled her and rubbed against her.
They were so friendly
that Gretchen was not afraid.
And she did not realize
that Anna had wandered
far from the wagon train.

Suddenly the horses
began to nibble
at the sacks on Anna's back.

They had smelled the corn meal.
In their eagerness
they nipped Gretchen's legs.
Gretchen screamed.
She tried to move out of the way.
She tried to loosen the ropes
that tied her.
But she could not reach the knots.
Terrified, Gretchen screamed
and screamed.

Out of nowhere
a great white stallion appeared.
He pranced and whinnied.
He swished his long white tail.
He stood on his hind legs,
his white mane flying.

The mares moved quickly
out of his way.
The white stallion
came up to Anna.
He carefully bit through the ropes
that tied Gretchen.

Then, gently, he took hold
of the back of her dress
with his teeth.
He lifted her to the ground.

He seemed to motion to the mares
with his head,
and then he galloped away.
The mares followed at once.
Anna followed them.

Gretchen was left alone.

She did not know what to do.
"Father will find me soon,"
she said out loud
to comfort herself.
She was hungry,
but there was nothing to eat.
She walked to the stream
and drank some water.
Then she sat down
on a rock to wait.

She waited and waited,
but there was no sign
of Father.
And no sign of Anna.
Shadows began to fall.
The sun went down.
The dark came.
"Anna!" Gretchen called.
"Anna! Anna! Anna!"

There was no answering sound.
She heard a coyote howl.
She heard the rustling
of leaves and
the call of redbirds.
Gretchen began to cry.

She made a place for herself
on some dry leaves
near a tree trunk.
She curled up against it,
and cried and cried
until she fell asleep.

Morning light woke Gretchen.
The stream sparkled
in the sunlight.
Gretchen washed her face
and drank the clear water.

She looked for Anna.
She called her name,
but Anna did not come.
Gretchen was so hungry
she chewed some sweet grass.
But it had a nasty taste,
and she spat it out.

She sat on her rock
near the stream.
She looked
at the red bite marks
on her legs
and began to cry again.

A squirrel came by.
It looked at her
in such a funny way
that she stopped crying.

She walked along the stream.
She knew she must not go far.
"If you are lost,"
Mother had warned,
"stay where you are.
That will make it easier
to find you."
Gretchen walked back
to her rock.

45

It was afternoon when she heard
the sound of hooves.
A moment later Anna
ambled up the stream.
The sacks of meal were gone.
The old mare drank greedily.
Gretchen hugged and kissed her.
She patted her back.
Anna would find her way
back to the wagon train.

She tried to climb on Anna's back,
but even without the sacks
the mare was too high.

There was a fallen tree
not far away.
Gretchen wanted to use it
as a step.
She tugged at Anna,
but Anna would not move.
Gretchen pulled and shoved.
She begged and pleaded.
Anna stood firm.

Now again
the white stallion appeared.
Again he lifted Gretchen
by the back of her dress.
He sat her on Anna's back.
He nuzzled and pushed
the old mare.
Anna began to walk.
The white stallion
walked close behind her
for a few paces.
Then, as if to say goodbye,
he stood on his hind legs,
whinnied, and galloped away.

51

Gretchen always believed
the white stallion had told Anna
to take her back
to the wagon train.
For that is what Anna did.

53

Your great-great-grandmother Gretchen
bore the scars of the wild mare bites
for the rest of her life.
I know because
when she told me the story,
she pulled down her stockings.
And I saw them.

ABOUT THE ILLUSTRATOR

Born and raised in New York City, RACHEL ISADORA studied at the School of American Ballet (associated with the New York City Ballet). She danced with the Boston Ballet until a foot injury forced her to consider another career—book illustration. "I had always drawn for my own entertainment," she says, "but I'd never had any instruction, and I wasn't sure how to proceed. So I just took a collection of sketches—odds and ends on bits of paper—to the first editor who would see me. She suggested I do a book about what I knew best." The result was *Max*, published in 1976 and named on ALA Notable Book. Since then, Rachel Isadora has written and illustrated *The Potters' Kitchen*, *Ben's Trumpet* (a Caldecott Honor Book and an ALA Notable Book), *My Ballet Class*, *"No, Agatha!"*, *Jessie and Abe*, and *The City Seen from A to Z*. She has also illustrated *Seeing Is Believing*, by Elizabeth Shub, and *Backstage*, which she wrote with Robert Maiorano. Rachel Isadora lives in New York City with her husband, James Turner, and young daughter, Gillian Heather.

CHOOSE YOUR OWN ADVENTURE

SKYLARK EDITIONS

☐ 15226	Jungle Safari #13	$1.95
☐ 15442	The Search for Champ #14	$2.25
☐ 15444	Three Wishes #15	$2.25
☐ 15465	Dragons! #16	$2.25
☐ 15489	Wild Horse Country #17	$2.25
☐ 15262	Summer Camp #18	$1.95
☐ 15490	The Tower of London #19	$2.25
☐ 15501	Trouble In Space #20	$2.25
☐ 15283	Mona Is Missing #21	$1.95
☐ 15418	The Evil Wizard #22	$2.25
☐ 15306	The Flying Carpet #25	$1.95
☐ 15318	The Magic Path #26	$1.95
☐ 15467	Ice Cave #27	$2.25
☐ 15342	The Fairy Kidnap #29	$1.95
☐ 15463	Runaway Spaceship #30	$2.25
☐ 15508	Lost Dog! #31	$2.25
☐ 15379	Blizzard of Black Swan #32	$2.25
☐ 15380	Haunted Harbor #33	$2.25
☐ 15399	Attack of the Monster Plants #34	$2.25
☐ 15416	Miss Liberty Caper #35	$2.25
☐ 15449	The Owl Tree #36	$2.25
☐ 15453	Haunted Halloween Party #37	$2.25
☐ 15458	Sand Castle #38	$2.25
☐ 15477	Caravan #39	$2.25
☐ 15492	The Great Easter Bunny Adventure #40	$2.25
☐ 15509	The Movie Mystery #41	$2.25
☐ 15517	Light On Burro Mountain #42	$2.25
☐ 15553	Home In Time For Christmas #43	$2.25
☐ 15565	You See the Future #44	$2.25

Prices and availability subject to change without notice.